The Invisible
Mix-Up

MerMicoRns

Sparkle Magic
A Friendship Problem
The Invisible Mix-Up

PuRRMaiDs

The Scaredy Cat
The Catfish Club
Seasick Sea Horse
Search for the Mermicorn
A Star Purr-formance
Quest for Clean Water
Kittens in the Kitchen
Merry Fish-mas
Kitten Campout
A Grrr-eat New Friendship

MeRMiCORns

3

The Invisible Mix-Up

by Sudipta Bardhan-Quallen

illustrations by Vivien Wu

A STEPPING STONE BOOK™

Random House New York

This is a work of fiction. Names, characters, places, and incidents either are the product of the author's imagination or are used fictitiously. Any resemblance to actual persons, living or dead, events, or locales is entirely coincidental.

Text copyright © 2021 by Sudipta Bardhan-Quallen
Cover art copyright © 2021 by Andrew Farley
Interior illustrations copyright © 2021 by Vivien Wu

Visit us on the Web!
rhcbooks.com

Educators and librarians, for a variety of teaching tools, visit us at
RHTeachersLibrarians.com

Library of Congress Cataloging-in-Publication Data
Names: Bardhan-Quallen, Sudipta, author. | Wu, Vivien, illustrator.
Title: The invisible mix-up / by Sudipta Bardhan-Quallen ;
illustrations by Vivien Wu.
Description: First edition. | New York : Random House Children's Books, [2021] |
Series: Mermicorns ; 3 | "A Stepping Stone book." | Audience: Ages 6–9. |
Summary: Mermicorns Serena and Lily try to use simple invisibility magic
while doing a school project about magical mistakes, and learn a powerful
lesson about using magic responsibly.
Identifiers: LCCN 2020043910 (print) | LCCN 2020043911 (ebook) |
ISBN 978-0-593-30879-0 (trade pbk.) | ISBN 978-0-593-30880-6 (lib. bdg.) |
ISBN 978-0-593-30881-3 (ebook)
Subjects: CYAC: Invisibility—Fiction. | Magic—Fiction. | Friendship—Fiction. |
Sisters—Fiction. | Librarians—Fiction. | Mermaids—Fiction. | Unicorns—Fiction.
Classification: LCC PZ7.B25007 Inv 2021 (print) | LCC PZ7.B25007 (ebook) |
DDC [Fic]—dc23

Printed in the United States of America
10 9 8 7 6 5 4 3 2 1
First Edition

This book has been officially leveled by using
the F&P Text Level Gradient™ Leveling System.

Random House Children's Books supports the
First Amendment and celebrates the right to read.

To Brooklyn,
the most thorough first reader under the sea

The Disappearing ART of INVISIBILITY

1

Sirena floated in front of the mirror. She checked her reflection. Her rainbow mane was beautifully brushed. She'd placed a sparkly silver hair clip in the perfect spot. The new pearl on her necklace looked lovely. She was all ready to leave for the Mermicorn Magic Academy. Except she couldn't leave yet. She was still waiting for Lily.

Sirena called out to the oyster garden

again. "Have you picked out an oyster yet, Lily?"

Lily shook her head.

Sirena sighed. Lily was a great best friend in so many ways. But she could be so slow when it was time to make a decision!

"I'm not like you, Sirena," Lily neighed. "I don't just pick something and move on."

"No, you take forever!" Sirena whined.

"I'm just trying to be careful so I don't make a mistake," Lily replied. She leaned over and finally chose an oyster. She opened it. Inside was a gigantic pink pearl!

She joined Sirena in front of the mirror. "See?" she exclaimed. "This was worth the wait!"

Sirena had to admit that Lily's pearl was nicer than the simple white pearl she'd found. "You're right," she said. "But I still wish you'd hurry."

Lily slid the pearl onto her necklace. The pink pearl looked wonderful against Lily's chestnut coat and her pink-and-purple mane.

"Are you ready to go now?" Sirena asked. "We're going to be late."

Lily nodded. Then she asked, "Do you have your permission slip?"

Sirena frowned. "No, I forgot to get it signed." She looked through her bag and took it out. "I don't understand why we need a permission slip to go to the library. It's just across the street from the Magic Academy."

"Well, if your parents are expecting you to be in one place and you're not," Lily replied, "they'd probably worry. What if you disappear?"

Sirena rolled her eyes. "Mermicorns don't just disappear," she muttered. She swam to the doorway and called for her mother. "I need you to sign something before we leave, Mom!"

"What is it?" Mom asked.

"Our class is visiting the library today," Sirena explained. "We'll be there until the end of the school day."

"My older sister works there," Lily

added. "My parents told me that we can stay at the library until Lotus is done. Then she will swim us home."

"That sounds like a great plan," Mom neighed. "I remember when I was a foal. I loved the library! There are so many books to get lost in."

Sirena smiled. "Do you want me to check out a book for us to read together?" she asked.

"That would be lovely," Mom said, "except that you don't always pay attention to what book you choose. Remember the last time? We had to read *A Guide to Mermicorn Skin Rashes*."

Lily giggled. "I bet she pretended she meant to choose that!"

Mom nodded. "She did! She can be very stubborn sometimes."

Sirena frowned. "If you two are done

squidding around, we should go," she said.

Mom floated over and kissed Sirena's forehead. "Have a great time at the library!"

The girls waved goodbye and swam toward the Magic Academy. Ms. Trainor was waiting outside today in the courtyard. Some students were already floating near her. Ms. Trainor was collecting permission slips. "Oh, good!" Lily said. "We're not late."

Sirena laughed. "You're lucky we aren't! I would be so mad if we missed the trip."

Sirena and Lily joined their classmates. As soon as the bell rang, Ms. Trainor took attendance. Then the class left for the library.

The Seadragon Bay Library was one of the most interesting buildings in town. From far away, it looked like a giant oyster with its mouth slightly open. When you swam closer, you could see that the mouth was really a wall of glass windows and doors. The roof and the sides of the building were shaped like the oyster's

shell. There were words carved above the central door. They read, THE WORLD IS YOUR OYSTER. IT'S UP TO YOU TO FIND THE PEARLS.

Sirena and Lily smiled at each other. Sirena exclaimed, "I think today is going to be really exciting!"

2

Ms. Trainor led her students to the main classroom at the back of the library. "It's the only place I can talk to you without getting into trouble," she whispered.

Mrs. Booker, the head librarian, overheard her, though. She spun around and said, "Shhhhhh!"

Sirena had wanted to laugh at what Ms. Trainor said. But Mrs. Booker wasn't the kind of mermicorn who liked jokes.

She was always very serious. Every time Sirena saw her at the library, her entire mane was pulled back into a tight bun. She wore a spotless white shirt buttoned all the way up to the top every day. Everything on her desk was stacked neatly, and she put books back on the shelves the moment they were returned. The only times Sirena had ever seen Mrs. Booker smile was when someone noticed the small sign on her desk. It said, A LIBRARIAN CAN ALWAYS FIND THE ANSWERS.

The students swam past bookshelves that stretched almost to the roof of the library. Sirena had been visiting the library since she was a tiny foal. She'd read many,

many books. Still, she knew that all the books she'd read wouldn't even fill one of the bookshelves. But that just meant Sirena had to keep reading!

When everyone was inside the classroom, Ms. Trainor shut the heavy door behind her. Then she let out a deep breath. "I'm glad I didn't get us into too much trouble!" she joked. She swam to the front of the room and floated to a large screen on the wall. "I'm so happy everyone is here today. Usually, there is at least one student who forgets their permission slip."

Lily elbowed Sirena. "That was almost you," she whispered.

Sirena stuck her tongue out at Lily.

"Today, we're going to talk about magic," Ms. Trainor continued.

Lily raised a hoof. "Don't we talk about magic every day?"

The students laughed.

Ms. Trainor smiled. "Yes, that's true. But today we're going to have a different kind of lesson than you're used to. We are going to learn a little about the history of mermicorn magic. There are many examples of mermicorns doing incredible things with magic. But there are also examples of mistakes that came from being careless." She pressed a button, and the screen behind her lit up. "This is a zigzag coral. It's one of my favorites. Unfortunately, Seadragon Bay is too warm for zigzag corals to grow." She flipped to a different picture. "This is the garden in the first house I had as a grown-up. I really wanted to have my own zigzag corals. So I used magic to make my garden icy cold." The next picture showed the same garden with a few small zigzag corals.

"You got them to grow!" Sirena said.

Ms. Trainor nodded. "I did. But look closely at the rest of the picture. Can you see anything wrong?"

The mermicorns studied the screen for a few moments. Then Lily raised her hoof. "The zigzag corals are the only things growing."

Ms. Trainor smiled again. "Exactly! I used magic to change something that

wasn't supposed to be changed. And I did more harm than good. All the fish, snails, crabs, and other creatures who lived in the corals that were supposed to be there had to find new homes. The only thing that would live in the garden was a cold-water octopus. I had to call animal control to come pick him up!"

The students laughed.

"Magic can give mermicorns a lot of power," Ms. Trainor continued, "which means we have to be responsible. If magic is used in the wrong way, it can cause big problems. Today, you'll be working with a partner to read about a type of magic. You'll end up learning many different things, but I want you to pay special attention to examples of magical mistakes. Let's see what we can learn from those mistakes!"

3

Sirena thought the project sounded fun. She whispered to Lily, "Other mermicorns' mistakes are always interesting."

Lily giggled.

Aqua raised her hoof. "Do they have to be big mistakes?" she asked.

Ms. Trainor shook her head. "Not at all! In fact, sometimes you can learn more from a small mistake than from a big one! Tomorrow we will share all your stories in class." She swam to the door and waved for the students to follow. "I'm going to take you down to the research part of the library," she said. "That's where you'll find the rarest nonfiction books about mermicorn magic and mermicorn history."

Sirena frowned. "Wait—there's a *down* to the library?" she asked.

The other students looked just as confused as Sirena. But Ms. Trainor grinned. "Oh, you are in for a treat!" she exclaimed. "Not every mermicorn gets to see the lower level of the library. You need special permission to go down there. Mrs. Booker was kind enough to set it up for us." She opened the door. Mrs. Booker was floating right outside. "Are you all ready for an adventure?" Ms. Trainor asked. "Follow us!"

The main floor of the library was

bright and cheerful. The rows of book-shelves were lined up perfectly. Sirena had spent hours and hours there, reading and learning. But the lower level was the complete opposite. Here, the shelves snaked and curved in every direction. Instead of sunlight shining down through skylights, the lower level was lit by lamps on every bookshelf. Sirena swam close to one of the lamps. Her eyes grew wide when she realized how they gave light. "These are glow-in-the-dark jellyfish!" she cried.

Mrs. Booker looked over her shoulder at Sirena. "Shhh!" she said. "This is still part of the library. Please be quiet."

"Thank you, Sirena," Ms. Trainor whispered.

"For what?" Sirena asked, quietly this time.

"Now I'm not the only one who got

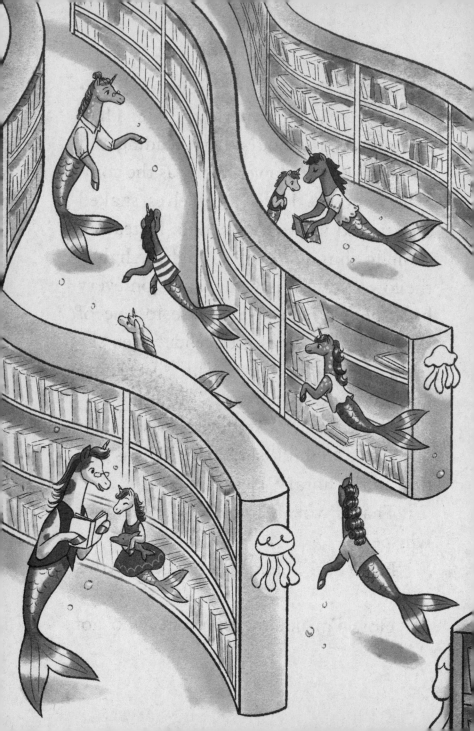

scolded for making too much noise!" Ms. Trainor replied.

Sirena covered her mouth with her hoof to keep from giggling too loudly.

Mrs. Booker led the students through a maze of shelves. Finally, they reached a larger, open area. She waited until the whole class had gathered. Then she said, "This is the most important part of the Seadragon Bay Library. Here is where we keep the rarest books about magic, history, and mermicorn life. I usually don't let foals as young as you come down here. But Ms. Trainor promised me that this class is responsible and serious, and that you will treat these books with respect."

The mermicorns nodded. Mrs. Booker turned to leave. But before she disappeared into one of the winding aisles, she looked back at the class. "Remember, if you haven't found the answer in a book," she said, "you haven't found the right book yet!"

Ms. Trainor gave each group a topic for their projects. Clyde and Russel got warming magic. Misty and Buttercup got teleporting magic. Aqua and Pepper got disguising magic.

Then Ms. Trainor floated to Sirena and Lily. She checked her notebook and said, "You two get to learn about invisibility magic. That's one of my favorites!"

"Yay!" Lily exclaimed. "I can't wait!"

"If we find an example of interesting

magic," Sirena said to Lily, "maybe we can try it."

Ms. Trainor said, "You don't need to worry about doing magic today. I just want you to learn about magic and all the things that could happen if we aren't responsible with it."

Sirena frowned. She and Lily practiced magic on their own all the time. *Ms. Trainor never said we* shouldn't *try magic,* she thought. *So maybe I'll find something we can play around with.*

The
Disappearing
& ART of
INVISIBILITY

4

The books on the lower level of the library were organized by type of magic. Each shelf had a sign. Sirena and Lily swam around until they saw the one that said INVISIBILITY.

There were many shelves of books in the section. "I don't know where to start," Lily said. "Maybe this one? Or this one?"

Sirena shrugged. "Just pick one that looks cool." She didn't bother to read all the book titles. She just grabbed the one that had the fanciest spine. "*The Disappearing Art of Invisibility*," she read. "*Discover Forgotten Magic.*" She turned the cover so Lily could see. "This sounds interesting!"

The girls sat down and began flipping through the pages. "There are fourteen different types of invisibility magic," Sirena said.

"I didn't know that," Lily replied.

"I wonder why we need so many," Sirena said.

"It's probably in the book," Lily said.

Sirena flipped to the next page. "It says here that 'all invisibility magic makes the target invisible.' That doesn't explain why there are so many types."

Lily snorted. "There's still a lot of book left! You haven't finished reading it." She got up from the table. "Before we find that answer, we need to work on our project." She went back to the shelf. After looking for a long time, she took out another two books. They were two parts of *Invisibility Through Mermicorn History*. "These might be more useful."

Sirena frowned. She didn't want to learn how *other* mermicorns used magic. She wanted to learn how to *do* magic! But Lily was right. They needed to finish the assignment. She closed her book and pushed it away.

Lily put one of the history books in front of Sirena. She sat down and opened the other one.

The fillies read quietly for a while. Then Lily giggled. "I just read about a mermicorn student who accidentally made his final exam invisible. He had to do the entire year of school over again!"

"I bet he learned how to use invisibility magic the right way after that!" Sirena replied.

"Actually," Lily neighed, "he never used invisibility magic again!"

"I found something, too," Sirena said. She slid the book closer to Lily. "It's about Tiger Shark Trench and why it's so dangerous."

Tiger Shark Trench was a place where mermicorns were never supposed to go. Tiger sharks lived there, which is how it got its name. There were also other scary sharks like hammerheads and blue sharks. But the most dangerous animal who lived in Tiger Shark Trench was supposedly a giant great white shark. No one had seen the great white in many years—but then again, no one really went to Tiger Shark Trench.

"It says here that many, many years ago, a mermicorn was swimming alone in Tiger Shark Trench. He swam into a great white shark, and he tried to make himself invisible to hide. Except he made the shark invisible instead! So now the shark can hunt without ever being seen."

"So did he get eaten by the shark?" Lily asked.

"It doesn't say," Sirena said. "But probably. I mean, how do you get away from an invisible shark?"

"But if he was eaten," Lily said, "who told all the rest of the mermicorns about the invisible shark?"

"That's a good point," Sirena said. "Do you think some of the stories about magical mistakes are made-up? Like, they make us learn them so we are sure to be careful using magic?"

Lily shrugged. "I don't know. I don't think Ms. Trainor would try to fool us."

"But what if she was fooled by the same stories when she was a foal?" Sirena asked. "Maybe magic doesn't make as many problems as grown-ups say it does. Maybe they just tell us that so we don't try magic without them." Her eyes grew wide. "Do you know what that means?"

Lily shook her head.

Sirena laughed. "That means we *can* try new magic today!"

5

Before Lily could say yes or no, Mrs. Booker's voice came over the loudspeaker. "Magic Academy students, please go to the main-floor classroom. You will be dismissed from there."

The girls hadn't realized how much time had passed while they were reading. "And we're not even done!" Lily exclaimed. She put the two history books back on the shelf. "I wish we could read more of these."

"And more of this one, too," Sirena said. She held the book she had found first.

Sirena and Lily swam back upstairs. They saw a line of mermicorns in front of the main desk waiting to check out books. The line wasn't moving. That's because the mermicorn behind the desk wasn't doing the checkouts. She was just looking at her shell phone screen—and ignoring everyone around her.

Sirena would've recognized that mermicorn anywhere. It was Lotus, Lily's sister. Lotus's coat was the same chestnut color as Lily's coat. In fact, she looked like a slightly bigger copy of Lily, except for their manes. Lily's mane was a mix of purples and pinks. Lotus's mane was bright bubble-gum pink. She wore a lot of sparkly hair clips in her mane. She was almost too bright to look at!

"I thought you said Lotus *worked* at the library," Sirena whispered.

Lily giggled. "She gets a little distracted by text messages."

Mrs. Booker noticed the long checkout line. She swam up to Lotus and cleared her throat. "Are you in charge of the desk today, Lotus?" she asked.

Lotus quickly shoved her phone into her pocket. "Sorry, Mrs. Booker," she mumbled.

Mrs. Booker touched Lotus's shoulder. "When something is your responsibility," she neighed, "you have to try to do a good job. I know you know that."

Lotus looked away. "I do," she said.

Sirena elbowed Lily. "Your sister is really brave," she whispered. "I think I'd cry if Mrs. Booker told me I was doing something wrong."

"She is a little scary, isn't she?" Lily replied.

Just then, Lotus saw the girls. Her eyes grew wide, and she looked embarrassed. She quickly turned to one of the mermicorns in line.

"She probably doesn't like that we saw what happened," Sirena whispered.

Lily nodded. "Let's get out of here before she gets mad at us."

Sirena and Lily returned to the classroom. Parents began to arrive to pick up their students. After everyone else had gone home, Ms. Trainor swam over to Sirena and Lily. "I'm going to take you girls to Lotus now," she said. "Your parents said she would be responsible for you."

Sirena and Lily grabbed their backpacks. As they swam to the desk, Lotus gave Ms. Trainor a big smile. But when she saw Sirena and Lily, Lotus's smile got a little smaller.

"I have a special delivery for you, Lotus," Ms. Trainor neighed.

Lotus rolled her eyes and said, "It's Silly Lily!"

"Don't call me that," Lily said, frowning.

"If I have to watch you two all afternoon," Lotus said, "I should get to make a few jokes."

"Jokes are supposed to be funny," Lily muttered. She stuck her tongue out at her sister.

"Now, girls, be nice," Ms. Trainor said.

"We're just squidding around," Lotus

said. She smiled sweetly at the teacher again. "Lily, you and Sirena can sit at that table so I can keep an eye on you."

Ms. Trainor had a few books to check out. Lotus began to help her. Lily swam to the far side of the table. She plopped down into a seat and crossed her arms.

Sirena sat down next to her best friend. "Are you all right?" she asked.

Lily sighed. "Yes. It's just that big sisters can be really annoying." She sighed again. "I really don't want to sit near her for the rest of the afternoon. I'd rather just disappear."

Sirena touched Lily's shoulder. "We'll think of something." Then she grinned. "Maybe we *should* try some invisibility magic!"

They both giggled. Then Lily said, "You know, that's not a bad idea. If we went back to the research library, we could get away from Lotus."

"And learn some magic?" Sirena asked.

"If you can convince Lotus to let us go downstairs," Lily said, "then I guess we can try."

"It's a deal!" Sirena exclaimed, laughing. "I have a plan."

6

Sirena got up from the table. She swam over to Ms. Trainor. "Excuse me," she said.

"Yes?" Ms. Trainor replied.

"Lily and I still have lots and lots of questions," Sirena said. "Who should we ask?"

"Well, Lotus is the mermicorn at the main desk," Ms. Trainor said. "I guess she's the one you can ask!"

Lotus's eyes seemed to narrow a bit. But she said, "Yes, of course. I'm here to answer questions." She smiled again.

Ms. Trainor waved goodbye. As soon as the teacher was out of sight, Lotus's smile completely disappeared. "I'm really busy," she said, "so you two need to stay out of my way."

"You know," Sirena said, "we could go back to the research library. The books down there have all the answers we need. Then we wouldn't bother you."

Lotus scratched her mane. "That could work,"

she said. "But you need permission to be downstairs."

"You could ask Mrs. Booker for us," Sirena suggested, grinning. "Please?"

"Can't you ask her yourselves?" Lotus said.

Sirena shook her head. "No way! Mrs. Booker is too scary!"

Lotus rolled her eyes. "Fine," she said. "Come with me."

Sirena and Lily swam behind Lotus. She led them through the library. "What is the plan?" Lily whispered.

"Lotus is going to get us permission to go back downstairs," Sirena replied.

Lily's eyes grew wide. "Really?"

Sirena nodded.

When the fillies found Mrs. Booker, she was re-shelving a stack of books. Instead of carrying the books, though,

Mrs. Booker was using magic! She pointed her horn at a book and then at a shelf. The book magically floated up to where it belonged.

"Wow!" Sirena exclaimed. "That's amazing!"

"Cleaning my room would be so much easier if I knew that magic," Lily said.

"I'm not asking Mrs. Booker for two things for you," Lotus said. "But if you ask, she might show you how to do it."

Both Sirena and Lily shook their heads.

Mrs. Booker still seemed a little frightening. "I'd be too afraid," Sirena said.

"It's up to you," Lotus said, and shrugged. "But you won't get to learn the magic if you don't ask for help."

Lotus floated behind Mrs. Booker and softly said, "Excuse me."

"Is everything all right?" Mrs. Booker asked.

Lotus nodded. "My sister and her friend would like to go downstairs again. Can they go?"

Mrs. Booker frowned. "Their teacher is gone," she said. "Who's going to take responsibility for them?"

"I will," Lotus replied. "I'm done working at the desk today. I have to update some things on the computer. But I can do that downstairs."

Mrs. Booker smiled. "It sounds like you've made a good plan. You have my permission to go to the research library."

"Yay!" Sirena cheered.

Mrs. Booker's smile disappeared like magic. "Shhh!" she said. "Quiet in the library, please."

"Sorry!" Sirena whispered.

The fillies swam away as quietly as possible, just in case Mrs. Booker was watching. Lotus sat down in front of one of the library computers. "I'm going to be working here," she said.

Sirena frowned. "But the invisibility books are way over there," she said, pointing.

"This is the computer I have to use," Lotus said. "I have to stay here."

"Do we have to stay with you?" Lily asked.

"Are you going to ask me annoying questions the whole time?" Lotus asked. "Go to the invisibility section. I'll come find you when I'm done." She turned to the computer screen. "Just don't do anything that could get you into trouble. Or get *me* into trouble!"

The two girls found their way back to the invisibility section. Sirena grabbed her book from earlier. "Let's find some magic to learn," she said.

"I can't believe I agreed to this," Lily said.

"We practice magic every day after school," Sirena said. "Why should today be different?"

"On the other days, someone has *taught* us magic to practice," Lily replied. "Today, you want us to try on our own. And Ms. Trainor didn't say we should try magic."

"She also didn't say we shouldn't try magic," Sirena neighed. "Besides, I thought we decided that some of the scary stories about problems with magic stretch the truth a bit. Remember the invisible shark story?"

Lily scratched her mane. "I guess. But they aren't completely made-up. We know there are definitely some risks to magic. That was our whole lesson today!"

"I know," Sirena said. "We won't try anything hard! And we won't try all fourteen types of invisibility magic." She grinned. "We'll just try one. You know that when we work together, we can do anything!"

7

Lily nodded. "You're right." She opened the book. "Maybe we could try the first one. That's probably the easiest."

Sirena snorted. "Easiest means most boring," she said. "My lucky number is seven. Let's try the seventh one!" She flipped to the page. "Are you ready?"

Lily put her hoof over the open pages. "We should really read the whole book before we try anything," she said.

"That would take too long!" Sirena whined. "I just want to try the magic quickly. We're going to be going home soon." She pointed back toward Lotus. "You don't want our babysitter to see this, do you?"

Lily shook her head. "No, let's do this without Lotus knowing." She put her backpack on the table across from the book. "Let's make my bag invisible."

Sirena nodded. She closed her eyes to find her sparkle. Then she opened her eyes so she could read the magic words:

INVISIBILITY SPELL

Manta tooth, dolphin ear, shimmer, glimmer, disappear!

She looked at the backpack. But it wasn't the backpack that was shimmering and glimmering. It was Lily!

"What's happening?" Lily asked.

"I don't know!" Sirena cried.

The sparkles from the magic wrapped around Lily's tail. They swirled faster and faster. Then they started to disappear.

But so did Lily's tail!

Sirena couldn't believe what she had

done. She stared at Lily, hoping that she could wish her friend's tail back.

"Hey, you made the magic work!" Lily exclaimed. "Except for one little mistake."

"How can you joke around at a time like this?" Sirena asked. "Do you feel all right?"

Lily shrugged. "I can't see my tail," she answered. "But I can still feel it." She looked down at her invisible tail. Soon,

there were bubbles near where Lily's tail fin should have been. "I'm flapping my fin to make those bubbles," she said. "So my tail still works."

Sirena let out a deep breath. "That's good to hear," she said.

"We probably should make it un-invisible, though," Lily said.

"Ummm, yeah!" Sirena replied. She giggled. Even when Lily was half gone, she could make Sirena laugh!

The girls huddled together to find something in the book that could fix Lily's invisible tail. They were concentrating so hard that they didn't hear anyone float toward them.

"Are you two ready to go home yet?" someone asked.

Sirena and Lily popped up from their

seats at the sound of the voice. "Lotus," Lily said, "we didn't think you'd be done so soon."

Lotus ignored that. Instead, she stared at Lily. "What happened to your tail?" she asked.

Sirena gulped. "I can explain," she said. "Don't be mad."

But Lotus didn't look mad. She grinned. "I have to tell my friends about this!" she exclaimed. She took her shell phone out and started typing messages.

Sirena and Lily looked at each other. Lily shrugged.

"Ummm, Lotus," Sirena said. "Do you know how to make Lily's tail un-invisible?"

"Just a second," Lotus neighed without looking up.

It felt like forever before Lotus put her phone away. "So what happened?" she asked.

"We were learning about invisibility magic today," Sirena explained. "We thought it would be fun to try one of the types of invisibility magic from this book. But it didn't work out the way we thought."

"You mean you didn't *see* this coming?" Lotus asked, laughing.

Lily smiled at the joke. But Sirena didn't think it was funny. "I'm really worried, Lotus. I'm going to find Mrs. Booker."

But Lotus floated to block Sirena's way. "You two are such babies," she snapped. "Let me see the book. I'll fix this."

"I don't know, Lotus," Sirena said. "If you don't actually know how to fix this, maybe we should ask Mrs. Booker for help."

"I've been learning magic for a lot longer than you have," Lotus said. "I can figure this out on my own." She flipped through the book. "This should work, I think." She pointed to a chapter called "Reappearing Magic." "Let me just find the magic words. . . ."

"Are you sure that's the right magic?" Lily asked. "You didn't read the whole chapter."

"That'll take too long!" Lotus replied.

Sirena frowned. *That's what I said before,* she thought. *And I was wrong to rush through the magic.* She opened her mouth to say something, but Lotus had already found her sparkle.

"Lobster claw, penguin tears," Lotus said, "make the missing reappear!"

Like before, a glittery cloud surrounded Lily. "Is it working?" Lily asked.

"I think so," Lotus answered. "But I need to concentrate!"

Sirena held her breath. She kept her eyes on Lily. At first, the sparkles swirling around Lily made it hard to see. But soon, the sparkles began to fade. It looked like Lily was floating in cloudy water. She was still there, but she was disappearing. Then Sirena blinked—and Lily was gone!

"Lily?" Sirena cried. "Where are you?"

"I'm right here," Lily replied.

Lily's voice was still coming from the same spot. Sirena swam a little closer.

"Ow!" Lily yelped. "Watch where you're swimming!"

Sirena gasped. "Lily! You're completely

invisible!" She spun around to face Lotus. "What did you do? You made it worse!"

Lotus covered her mouth with her hoof. Her eyes grew wide. She just stared

at the spot where Lily was supposed to be for a moment. Then she gasped. "I don't know what happened!" she exclaimed. "I thought that would work!"

"Well, it didn't!" Lily cried. "Now what do we do?"

Lotus was already looking through the book again. "I'm trying to see if there's something else we can try."

The girls sat down to read the book together. But Sirena was having a hard time. She couldn't really pay attention when she was this upset. The words on the page stopped making sense. Her eyes began to fill with tears.

Just then, Lotus slammed the book shut. "This isn't going to work," she said. She frowned. "I think we have to find Mrs. Booker."

"Won't she be mad?" Lily asked.

Lotus shrugged. "Maybe. But I don't know how to figure this out."

Sirena sighed. "That means it's time to ask a librarian." Even if that was a terrifying thought!

8

The library was almost empty when the fillies swam back to the main floor. They found the head librarian sitting behind the main desk. She was working on the computer. Her face looked very serious.

As soon as Sirena saw Mrs. Booker, she felt butterfly fish in her tummy. *Maybe we shouldn't ask her for help,* she thought. *She'll definitely be angry.*

Suddenly, Sirena wished *she* could

disappear. But it was too late. Mrs. Booker had noticed the girls.

"Hello, Lotus," Mrs. Booker said. "I see Sirena. But where's your sister Lily?"

Lotus and Sirena gulped at the same time. Neither one really wanted to answer that question. But they didn't have to. Lily neighed, "I'm right here!"

"Where?" Mrs. Booker asked. "I don't see you."

"That's the problem!" Lily exclaimed.

At first, Mrs. Booker looked confused. But then her mouth opened slowly and she nodded. "Every year," she said, "there's at least one research group who gets into a bit of a mess. Am I correct that you need help?"

Sirena and Lotus nodded. Lily did, too—there were little bubbles to prove it.

"So, I'm guessing your group was

supposed to study invisibility magic?" Mrs. Booker asked.

The mermicorns nodded again.

"And you decided to do something irresponsible and try magic without help?" Mrs. Booker asked.

"It was my fault," Sirena cried. "It was my idea, and I shouldn't have made Lily do it."

"No," Lotus said, "it was my fault. I was supposed to be watching them. I didn't do a good job of it." She bit her lip. "And I made things worse."

"How?" Mrs. Booker asked.

Lotus looked down at her tail. "Sirena and Lily only managed to turn half of Lily invisible," she said. "I told them I could fix it. Even though I don't know how." She wiped away a tear. "I was trying to show off. But I just made *all* of Lily invisible!"

Mrs. Booker floated over and put a hoof on Lotus's and Sirena's shoulders. "Like I said, you are hardly the first students to make a mistake like this," she said. "I'm glad you decided to get some help. Let's see what we can do. Tell me exactly what happened."

Sirena nodded. She handed the librarian the book from downstairs. "We found this book. I thought it would be fun to try some magic." She flipped to the right page. "I wanted to make Lily's backpack invisible with this," she said, pointing.

Mrs. Booker read quickly. She frowned. "This magic only works on other living creatures," she said. "It couldn't work on the backpack. Instead, it worked on the closest living thing."

Sirena gulped. "I didn't know that."

"Did you read all the warnings?" Mrs. Booker asked. "There's a whole chapter of them at the end of the book."

"We didn't read that far," Lily said.

Mrs. Booker sighed. "And how about

you, Lotus?" she said. "What did you try that made things worse?"

Lotus found the page and showed the librarian. "I thought this would make Lily reappear."

"You mixed invisibility magic?" Mrs. Booker gasped.

"I don't know," Lotus replied. "I didn't even think about that."

Mrs. Booker turned to the chapter on warnings. "It says right here, 'Never mix different types of invisibility magic. This could create an unstable situation.'" Mrs. Booker looked at Sirena and Lotus. "It also says, 'Invisibility magic can be tricky. Always have an experienced mermicorn supervising new magic students,'" she continued. She looked at the girls again. "Did you have someone supervise you?"

The fillies shook their heads.

Mrs. Booker sighed. "I understand that you're at the age when rules seem boring. But the rules are there for a reason."

"We're really sorry," Sirena said. She glanced over at where Lily was supposed to be. Her heart hurt because she couldn't see her best friend. She pointed to the sign on Mrs. Booker's desk as she read it aloud. " 'A librarian can always find the answers.' So can you fix this?"

Mrs. Booker shook her head. "I can't," she said. "You girls need to fix it yourselves."

Sirena felt tears forming in her eyes. "But we don't know how to fix it!" She looked down at her tail. "I've made a mess of everything."

"It's all right, Sirena," Lily said. But hearing her friend's voice without being

able to see her was even worse for Sirena.
She started to cry.

"Isn't there anything you can do, Mrs.
Booker?" Lotus asked.

"Of course there is," Mrs. Booker
replied.

Sirena's mouth fell open. "What?" she
gasped. "You just said you couldn't fix
this!"

"I can't fix it," Mrs. Booker answered. "But I can show you how to fix it."

Sirena's mouth hung open. "You *do* know how to fix this?" she asked. "Why didn't you just say so!"

"Because that isn't the question you asked," Mrs. Booker said, grinning. "Words matter. If you don't use the right words, you may not get the result that you want." She waved for the mermicorns to come closer. "I'll show you where to find the answer."

9

Mrs. Booker opened the book to the last chapter. "You girls gave up too easily," she said. She pointed to a paragraph.

" 'What to do when there's an invisibility mishap,' " Lily read. "What's a *mishap*?"

"A mishap is an unfortunate accident," Mrs. Booker replied.

"That's definitely what happened here," Lotus said.

"'If invisibility magic needs to be reversed,'" Lily continued, "'only the mermicorns involved in the original mishap can make things right.'"

"That's why you can't do it for us, Mrs. Booker," Sirena said.

Mrs. Booker nodded. "But the magic words are here. One of you has to do the magic. I'll be here to help in any way that I can." She looked at Sirena and Lotus. "Which one of you girls wants to try?"

Sirena swam forward. She read the magic words from the book. Then she closed her eyes to try the magic. "Squidworm, batfish, coral tree, what was hidden, show to me!"

But it didn't work. "I'm too upset to find my sparkle," Sirena said.

Lotus tried next. "I think I'm too upset, too," she said.

"Now what do we do?" Sirena asked.

"I'm sure Ms. Trainor taught you that it's all right to be upset," Mrs. Booker neighed. "You should talk through your feelings. That might help you find your sparkle." She smiled. "Is there anything else you're feeling?"

"I just feel invisible," said Lily's voice. It trembled a little like she was trying not to cry.

"That probably doesn't feel very positive," Mrs. Booker said.

"No," Lily mumbled.

Lotus looked down at her tail. "I feel guilty that I tried to do something I didn't know how to do," she said. "I feel awful about not paying enough attention when I was reading. But I really do want to fix this. You're my sister, Lily. I love you. I never want to stop seeing you."

Sirena floated toward Lily's voice. "I love you, too, Lily," she said. "You're my best friend. I'm so sorry I got you into this mess. I would do anything to make it right." Sirena closed her eyes and covered her face with her hooves. She couldn't look at Lily anymore—not when she couldn't see her face!

Then Sirena heard Mrs. Booker's voice. "Look, girls," she said.

Sirena opened her eyes. She could tell that her horn was glittering a little bit. Lotus's horn was glittering, too. But there was something else. Someone else's horn was sparkling—more brightly than Sirena had ever seen. *It must be Lily's horn!* Sirena couldn't see her friend, but she could see that she had found her sparkle!

"Do you remember the magic words, Lily?" Mrs. Booker asked.

The sparkles moved up and down. Lily was nodding.

Lily said, "Squidworm, batfish, coral tree, what was hidden, show to me!"

At first, nothing happened. Then Sirena

saw a mermicorn-sized part of the water begin to sparkle. "Lily!" she yelped. She floated closer. The sparkles got brighter. Then, like before, they started to swirl. Sirena held her breath. *Please let this work,* she thought.

For the longest time, it felt like nothing else was happening. Lotus floated closer to hold Sirena's hoof. Together, they watched carefully.

Lily started to giggle. "This tickles!" she exclaimed.

"We still can't see her," Sirena whispered. "What if this is the wrong magic, too?"

"Be patient," Mrs. Booker said. "Just keep watching."

Suddenly, all the sparkles disappeared. But there was no Lily! "It didn't work," Lotus whispered.

Sirena couldn't hold the tears back anymore. She and Lotus hugged each other while they both sobbed.

Someone tapped Sirena's shoulder. "Can I get a hug, too?" Lily asked. "I'm right here."

Sirena turned her head toward Lily's voice. Then she gasped. "Lily! I can see you!"

"You're not invisible anymore!" Lotus added.

"What did I tell you?" Mrs. Booker asked, laughing. "Librarians can always find the answer!"

10

"I can't believe you made the magic work, Lily!" Sirena exclaimed.

"I know!" Lily replied. "But you and Lotus made it so easy to find my sparkle. I don't think I could have done it without your help."

"How did we help?" Lotus asked. "All we did was apologize."

"Sometimes, taking responsibility for what you've done and saying you're sorry are the best things you can do to help someone else," Mrs. Booker said. "Now, are you girls ready to go home?"

Sirena and Lily nodded. "I've spent enough time in the library today!" Lily said.

"I don't think we need to read about mistakes mermicorns make with invisibility magic ever again," Sirena said, giggling. "I think we can tell the class about what we did here today!"

"It's very brave of you to be willing to share your mistake," Mrs. Booker said. "And I think your classmates will learn a good lesson from you. I'm proud of you!"

"Make sure you tell them how I helped you!" Lotus said. Mrs. Booker turned to look at her. She raised an eyebrow. Lotus shrugged. "I guess you can tell them about my little mistake, too."

"Actually," Sirena said, "I *will* tell them how you helped. We'll tell our class how you did everything you could to make things better for your little sister."

"It's just that you couldn't do much," Lily teased. She rushed to hug her sister, though, so Lotus wouldn't be upset. "Thank you, Lotus."

"I know I tell you to get lost all the time," Lotus said. "But I would be really sad if that actually happened."

"Well, girls, I have some more work to do," Mrs. Booker neighed. "So maybe it's time for the three of you to disappear." She winked. "The old-fashioned way!"

The three fillies were about to leave the library when Sirena stopped. "I need a minute," she said. "I have to do one more thing." She swam back to the main desk.

"Did you forget something, Sirena?" Mrs. Booker asked, frowning.

Sirena nodded. "I wanted to thank you again for helping us today. It was our mess, but we couldn't have cleaned it up without you."

Mrs. Booker smiled. "That's what mermicorns like me are here for, Sirena.

To help you foals learn how to be responsible grown-ups. Small mistakes shouldn't ruin anyone's life. You should learn from them. And you should always ask for help when you need it to make things right."

"You're very smart," Sirena said. She grinned. "I also wanted to tell you that you're not as scary as I thought you were. I should have gotten to know you before I decided what kind of mermicorn you are!"

"Shhh!" Mrs. Booker said. "Don't let anyone hear you!" She winked again. "There are some things mermicorns should learn for themselves!"

Lotus and Lily swam Sirena back to her house. It had been a long day. But there was still something Sirena needed to do.

When they reached the oyster garden, Sirena took Lily's hoof. "You have to pick out a new pearl for your necklace," she said. "You deserve it."

Lily realized what Sirena meant. "I couldn't have done it without you," she said. "You helped me find my sparkle. We both should get pearls."

Sirena shook her head. "You learned the magic that fixed my mistake today. Lotus and I couldn't do it. I'm glad I was able to help you, but you are the only one who gets a pearl today. I have to wait." She smiled. "I'm not going to stop trying until I catch up to you!"

Together, the girls picked out an oyster. There was a silver pearl inside. Sirena helped put it on Lily's necklace.

Lily hugged Sirena. "You're a really great friend," she whispered.

"And you're very talented," Sirena whispered back.

Then Lotus said, "Aren't you two forgetting something?"

Sirena frowned. Maybe Lotus was jealous that she didn't get to pick out an oyster, too? "The pearls are something we get when we learn magic, Lotus," she explained. "But you can have one if you want."

Lotus grinned. "That's very nice of you," she said. "But that's not what I mean. You're not finished with everything that you need to do yet."

"You're right," Lily neighed. "We still have to figure out how to tell the class about our adventure this afternoon."

"I can help you, if you want," Lotus said. "And no magic this time, I promise!"

Sirena and Lily laughed. Then Lily said, "We should get started. We don't have a lot of time."

"I'm not worried!" Sirena exclaimed. "When we work together, we can do anything!"

Oh no! Lily has the sniffles.
Does that mean she'll miss out
on fun with her friends?

Read on for a sneak peek of the next
Mermicorns adventure!

When Mom knocked on her door, Lily was still upset. She didn't want to look at anyone. She grabbed her blanket and pulled it over her head.

Mom swam over to the bed. "I know you're not feeling well," she neighed. "I bet your head hurts from the fever."

Lily nodded.

"And your throat hurts from sneezing and coughing," Mom added.

Lily nodded again.

Mom gently pulled the blanket back. "And," she said, "I bet your heart hurts from disappointment."

Lily gulped. "I really wanted to see everyone at the clubhouse this afternoon," she mumbled.

"I know, Lily," Mom said. She patted Lily's hoof.

"I don't feel that bad," Lily muttered. "Dad is being way too careful."

"He's a doctor, Lily," Mom said. "If there's any mermicorn who knows what to do, it's him!"

"Can't Dad use magic to make me better?" Lily asked.

"Any parent in the world would make their children magically feel better if they could," Mom replied. "So if there is something we're *not* doing, it's because it isn't possible. There are just some things that magic can't do. Making a cold or a fever go away is one of them."

Lily frowned. "It's not fair! Are mermicorns trying to fix this?"

Mom nodded. "There are many mermicorn scientists who work very hard to find treatments for every kind of illness," she said.

"Is science the same as magic?" Lily asked.

Mom giggled. "Science can certainly feel magical! Sometimes, when someone doesn't understand all the science, it might make them think it's just all magic. But science is real, and it does wonderful things for the world."

"So if I can't go to school, what am I supposed to do all day?" Lily mumbled.

"You're supposed to rest," Mom said. "The more you take care of yourself now, the faster you'll get better." She smiled. "I do have some good news, though."

"What is—" Lily started.

Ding dong! Someone was at the door!

Mom smiled. "I wonder who that could be," she said. "Maybe Sirena?"

Lily frowned. "Why would Sirena be here?"

"Let's find out," Mom neighed. She floated to the door of Lily's bedroom. Sirena swam up and said, "Good morning, Mrs. Farrier. Can I talk to Lily for a minute?"

"Of course you can talk to her," Mom said. "It's just important that you stay a safe distance away from her. We don't want you to catch any germs Lily might have."

Sirena waved from the doorway. "How are you feeling?" she asked.